The Rainbow Serpent

by

Lyra Shanti

Dedicated to my beloved soul-mate, Timothy. You are my garden, and my rainbow. Special thanks to Juniper for the constant support and beautiful artwork. May the rainbow stay inside us all, no matter the gray world of illusion.

Innocence

In the beginning, the word for Creation was "Al" or "Om," or even to some, "Ah."

It was a sound... a feeling... a dream.

Some did not even dare give it a name, for the language of Creation was impossible to decipher or translate. Yet, it was the oldest, most common language between all living beings, and even some of the animals in the forests and jungles had heard its universal sound.

It was divine and incomprehensible. It was the truth of all truths; the sound... the feeling... the dream.

The animals were the first to hear it. They awakened in the dark of night, listening to the sound of the rushing rivers and the pounding heartbeats of their newborn children.

"Listen!" cried the Queen of the Elk. "Listen to the rain as it falls from the sky! It is the sound of the heavens!"

"It must be magic, Mother!" replied her eldest calf.

"Yes," she said with a knowing smile, "it is indeed magic."

Then the King of the Lions heard it too!

"Feel!" roared the ferocious, but loving king. "Feel the wind as it blows through your fur! Feel how it caresses you, as if the wind itself was your own mother!"

Then all the lions roared with him, feeling the wind... becoming one with the holy truth of their emotions.

Gradually, the sounds and feelings of Creation covered the great plains, forests, and jungles everywhere, and all the animals above and below the ocean were caught up in the silent, singular dream: The Dream of Love.

Then, one day, the sleeping serpent woke up from his own dream. It was similar to the dream that all the animals were sharing, but it was different somehow—clearer and more intense. In fact, he was so excited from the immense feeling that he leapt down from his favorite tree and slithered as quickly as he could to tell his friends what he had seen and heard in his amazing dream!

"My friends!" he happily shouted. "My dearest friends, I must tell you about my wonderful dream!"

First, he went over to the watering hole where the elephants gathered. He knew they, with their wisdom and intelligence, would understand and truly listen.

"Oh, great creatures, I have seen such wonders! Would you like to hear about my amazing dream?"

Nodding, the wisest and oldest of the elephants said, "Why, yes, dear snake, I would love to hear about your dream. What mysteries did it show you?"

"Well," said the serpent, still catching his breath from the excitement, "when it began, it was just clouds... and then rain. But soon after, the clouds cleared, and the sky turned colors! So many colors, dear shaman, that my head felt as if it would burst with ideas!"

"Really?" said the shaman of elephants as he stopped drinking for a moment to gather his thoughts. "What kind of colors?"

"All kinds!" the serpent nearly shouted. "I saw pink and blue and yellow and red! I even saw colors in between! And it arched over the clouds, as if covering the whole world with its love and protection! It made me so happy! I felt warm and safe – like I have never been alone, and never will be again! And now I want to tell everyone everywhere about it so they may feel the same love and warmth!"

"That is wonderful, lively serpent, but I wish I could have seen it as well. The sky is always changing, it is true, but to see such a display of color would be so very moving, even if only from a dream. I have a feeling you were gifted with your dream for a reason. You must feel very lucky."

"I do feel lucky, but what do you mean? What reason would I have for being gifted with seeing colors?"

"I do not know, lucky snake, but I have a feeling you will figure it out soon. Dreams are special things, and your dream seems even more so. I very much like it, and I think you should tell all the animals how they are not alone. The sky itself seems to want you to spread the word."

"Yes!" the serpent happily agreed. "I WILL spread the word! Thank you, wise shaman, I will go now and tell all the animals about the colors in the sky! It is my destiny!"

Soon, the serpent slithered away to tell the Queen of the Elk, the King of the Lions, and any other animal who would listen to his incredible dream. He was so filled up with excitement, he even braved telling the great Emperor of the Ocean: The Lord of the Whales!

Standing on a tall, jagged rock, the serpent stretched his body as far as it would go so he could see where the Great Whale was swimming. When he saw him, he yelled, "Oh, Great Whale Lord, I must speak with you! It is a story that you must hear!"

Suddenly, the Whale Lord breached his head out of the water, creating a tidal wave that almost knocked the serpent backward off the rock! "What kind of story?" asked the Whale Lord with his vibrating, deep voice as he dove back into the ocean.

Realizing the Whale Lord would not easily listen to him, the crafty and brave snake took a deep breath and dove into the sea. "Wait, Whale Lord!" he gurgled under the water. "My story is very important! It is about my dream of colors and how we are all under its love and protection!"

Turning to face the small snake, the huge lord of whales said, "The colors? Do you speak of the light that pours into the water when the sun shines?"

"Well... yes, and no," said the snake, still holding his breath.

"Here, let me help you," said the Whale Lord. "Jump on my back, and tell me the story while we ride on the water for a while. I will listen as I survey my vast ocean. I must make sure all is well with my subjects, but I can listen to you at the same time."

Telling the Great Whale Lord about the vast sky, the rain, and the vibrant array of colors that emerged afterward, the snake felt even more impassioned than ever as he rode the waves on top the giant whale. It felt to him as if the dream took on even more importance as the cool droplets of water splashed his smooth, pale face. He smiled and breathed in the fresh, ocean air. *I am so alive!* He thought as he waited for The Whale Lord to say something about his story.

After a few moments of silence, the Whale Lord finally said, "Hmm... that is indeed a great dream. I'm curious, little snake, what did the other animals have to say when you told them?"

"Well," said the snake as he relaxed on the Whale Lord's back, "The Shaman of the Elephants was very interested and told me to talk about it to everyone. So I did, but The King of the Lions said he had already felt warmth from the sun, and that he'd never seen any colors like in my dream. And the Elk Queen said that the trees gave her protection, and that is enough for her. No one really understood how important my dream was. It made me sad... but it also made me want to speak with you even more. Everyone says that you're the smartest and oldest creature under the sky!"

The Whale Lord knowingly smiled and said, "Yes, I am very old, that is true... and I do think about a great many things in a way that most may not. I have a large kingdom, you see, deep under the ocean, and I must keep an eye at all times on my fellow water beings."

"Yes, it must be very difficult being their protector."

"Not as difficult as it must be for the sky, if it truly is protecting us the way you think it might be."

"Well... I'm not sure," said the snake, "but I felt a great sense of warmth and hope... as if the colors themselves meant that the sky cares in some way. It was... oh, I don't know, maybe this is silly, but..."

"Yes?" coaxed the Whale Lord. "Go on..."

Gathering his nerve, the serpent said, "It felt as if the colors were showing me that we are all connected somehow and that something new and amazing is coming soon to teach us how to be as connected as the colors in the sky!"

A great big smile spread across the Whale Lord's face. "Yes..." he replied, "I think your dream may indeed be a sign."

"A sign? What do you mean?" asked the snake, who was beginning to shiver from the sprinkles of water, as well as from their conversation.

"Sometimes, little snake, Alomah shows us signs to give us direction and truth. Sometimes we see them in dreams, sometimes in shadows in the air. But when we see them or hear them, it is always because Alomah wanted it that way."

"Alomah?" asked the shivering serpent. "What is Alomah?"

"It is the ancient word for Creation. We are all a part of it, little snake, and I believe it gave you that dream for a grand purpose."

"What sort of grand purpose?" whimpered the snake. Realizing the serpent was freezing cold, the Whale Lord swam up to the jagged rocks and let the snake warm up on the rock.

"Only you can figure that out," said The Whale Lord, "but I think you already know. Like you said, the colors are showing you something new is coming – something we've never known before, and I for one am very excited to see what happens!"

With that, the Great Whale Lord jumped back into the ocean, showing his joy with a giant thrash of his tail. It was awe-striking and made the serpent wish he too had a large tail for swimming. His own tail was slender and smooth, not big and wide. He imagined he could swim if he really tried, but he knew he couldn't splash and swim the way the whales and sea creatures did. He envied them, but he also knew he could do things they couldn't – like slither quickly through the sand to escape danger or shed his skin when he felt the need to grow.

I guess we all have our unique strengths, he thought as he warmed up from the sun. *And besides, I'm the one who has had this amazing vision! And I will be the one to see it when the wonderful new thing happens to show us how to be more connected, I just know it!*

Warmed and energized, the pale serpent stretched and slithered toward his favorite tree. He was famished, so he took his usual curled position in the tree and waited for a meal to present itself. He wasn't feeling sleepy, but he closed his eyes. Meditating in the moment, the serpent yawned—alert, yet waiting for something to tempt his hunger.

A few hours went by before the serpent woke from his meditation. He had heard a rustling in his tree and smelled something sweet, yet salty nearby. He hoped it was a mouse or a lizard, but instead, it was something much bigger and much more strange looking. In fact, as he adjusted his eyes to see the thing more clearly, he realized he had never seen such an odd creature in all his life!

She was far bigger than a mouse, and she was sitting down by the root of his tree, resting in the shade. Utterly intrigued, the snake sat and watched her. She had dark brown hair that flowed down to her back; it was wavy hair – thick and soft. He watched her as she sighed and rubbed her stomach. He had never seen such a stomach! It was round and big, and seemed to be radiating extra energy. It made his nostrils widen as his curiosity peaked.

Unable to control his urge to see her better, he slowly slithered down his tree. He had been born very near to his tree and had never shared it with anyone before. As far back as he could remember, the large tree with its overreaching branches and deep roots had always been all his, but now... the woman with long hair seemed to be laying claim to it as well.

She moaned and put up her hand to block the rays of the sun. *Why would she do that?* thought the curious, though confused snake. *Doesn't she like the warmth of the sun? Maybe she's sick? Her stomach is so big! Maybe she ate too much and can't move! I've done that on occasion, and it's not enjoyable. Maybe I should help the poor thing. I know she is very different than I, but maybe she won't mind if I talk to her. She seems so fragile. I doubt she would turn me away if I spoke in kind, sincere words.*

So the snake slithered even closer to the woman. She did not notice, however, since she had her eyes closed and seemed preoccupied with rubbing her stomach.

"Excuse me, but are you in trouble? Do you need any help?" asked the pale snake who was now hanging on the lowest branch in order to be eye level with the woman. She didn't reply, nor opened her eyes. *Hmm... maybe she can't hear me. I should speak louder.*

Trying again, the brave snake said, "Excuse me! Are you hurt? Can I help you? I know a lot about over eating and..." He would have continued talking, but he could tell the woman didn't understand a word he was saying. *I guess we speak two very different languages.*

Disappointed, the serpent resigned to simply watching the woman as she rested in the shade of the tree.

He was still famished, but in his curiosity, he forgot about his hunger. He had never seen such a mystifying creature! He noticed she had lightly tan skin, but she wore some sort of extra skin on certain parts of her body. The extra skin looked like his own skin – pale and smooth. He wondered why she wore it. *Is she somehow still cold in this sun? Does she like my skin and wishes to be like me? There must be a reason! If only I could speak with her! I have so many questions!*

Then, to his surprise, the woman slowly opened her eyes and looked straight at him. Nervous, he shifted his body a little, causing him to hang down a bit closer to where she sat.

"Um... hello," he said shyly.

The woman raised her brow and smiled. "Hello, snake," she spoke in a sweet voice. To him, it sounded like music, almost like the song of rain with its pitter-patter rhythm. "I hope you're not going to eat me," she added, "because if so, I have to warn you, I am with child, and we may be too much of a meal."

A bit off-set by her bluntness and strange sense of humor, he took a moment to respond. "Oh! Of course!" he finally replied. "You're pregnant! Don't worry, I don't want to eat you. I would never do that to someone I just met, especially when they are so interesting and different."

She nodded, grinning, and said, "No, you would have done it by now if you had desired. Perhaps you are here instead to keep me company through the birth. It will happen any moment, dear snake... and I confess, I am a little frightened."

The snake wasn't sure if she could understand his words or not, but they seemed to be conversing nonetheless. It made him hopeful and excited to speak with his new, exotic friend.

"Yes," he sympathized, "it is understandable to be frightened of something so arduous. But... birth is a wonderful thing! I have seen many animals do it, and if they survive, they seem so happy afterward!"

Turning her head, she sighed and said, "Oh, snake... if only my husband could be here with me. He is a good man, you see, but he is blinded by tradition. His father, and his father before him, planted the seed of superstition into my husband's mind. They believe that if he were present during the birth, he might bear witness to the mystery of life, and thereby offend the Creator who made us all. I know, snake... it is silly, but it is the way our people have lived for many years. Such traditions with no basis in reality have no hold over me. They never have, but I am different than most, I suppose."

Suddenly, she winced and grabbed onto the branch where the snake hung. He fell onto the ground, but being a bouncy snake, he gathered himself up and slithered to her side.

"Are you alright?" he asked the woman who was clearly in pain.

"I will be fine," she said through gritted teeth, "for I believe in the goodness of the universe, and I know that this child was meant to be here with me."

The snake was awestruck as he watched the brave woman give birth. She moaned, then stretched her legs wide apart so that the child could have plenty of room. The snake wondered if she had done this before or if her instinct was telling her what to do. Either way, he was quite impressed.

As she began to sweat, she panted and became flushed. "Oh, Great Mother," the woman shouted to the sky, "please give me strength!" Seeming as if she could no longer deal with the pain, the woman swayed and closed her eyes. The snake worried she might faint!

"I'm here!" cried the snake, hoping to catch her if she fell. She didn't seem to hear him, so he decided to take matters in his own scales and quickly slithered up his tree. *There's water in the leaves, I know it!* he thought. Hurriedly, he slid toward a large leaf and grabbed it with his tail. He yanked it off the tree, then carefully brought it down to the woman in labor.

"Here!" he shouted to the woman. "Open your mouth!"

She didn't open her mouth very much, but in her labor pains, she yelled with her face toward the leaf. At that exact moment, the snake squeezed the leaf and forced the water droplets to fall into her mouth. *It worked!* He thought as he raced back up the tree to get another giant leaf.

Soon, he had given the woman enough water to help her stay hydrated through the birth. She pushed and pushed and pushed until the snake heard a baby's cry. It was alive! It was a boy!

The snake was suddenly overcome with joy and relief, and he began to cry along with the child. He felt dizzy, but he was happy. *Is this what birth is really like?* he pondered as he rested at the base of the tree. *I have seen animals give birth before, but... somehow, this time was different. I was more a part of it, and I felt it as if I was going through it with her! I wonder why?*

While the serpent contemplated his feelings, the woman reached up to his face and pet his smooth cheek. "Thank you so much, my friend," she softly spoke while holding her newborn son. "I will never forget how you helped me and my child. I will even name him after you, if you don't mind."

The snake was filled with happiness and pride! "I would be honored!" he nearly yelled as he danced around her.

"Of course, I don't know your name," she said with a smile. "Would you tell me?"

Thinking for a moment, the snake realized he didn't have a name – not the kind she was asking for. "I... don't know what my name is," he replied, embarrassed.

"Hmm..." she whispered while nursing her son, "let me think. You are a kind and caring serpent, which most people do not realize even exist. Most think of snakes as terrible, sneaky creatures who bite and poison without thought. They have no idea how helpful snakes can be. I think I will name you something that represents the way you helped us. You were like the tree here with its strong branches and leaves, keeping us safe and cool. Yes, I think I will name you White Tree. What do you think, my sweet snake?"

"I love it!" said the snake as he swayed with glee.

"I will talk to my husband about how you helped us. I'm sure he will be happy to name his son after you."

The serpent danced and sang. He had never felt so alive! *Is this what being a parent feels like?* He silently asked. *If so, I can't wait to be one!*

Watching the woman breastfeed, he felt a surge of love for her, and he hoped she would visit again soon – with her son, and maybe even her husband. The snake was skeptical of her husband, however.

What kind of creature is scared of witnessing their child being born? he wondered. *He must be a little confused. I wish I could help him, but I suppose it is not my place. I should stay by my tree where I belong.*

He wanted to know her name, for if she were to return, he could call her by it. He also wanted to tell others of her beauty. "May I ask what your name is?" he asked, shyly, not knowing if she would even understand his question.

"My name means Lovely Garden," she replied, as if she heard him perfectly, "but you may call me Eden, for that is what my people call me in our language."

"Your name is beautiful, Eden," he said with a smile. "And how do you say my name in your language?"

"You would be called Alon."

It made the snake so happy to have his very own human name! He licked the air and danced in a circle.

"Wait," said the snake, stopping mid-dance, "do you actually hear and understand what I am saying?"

"Yes, I think I can," she replied. "I don't know why, but I can speak with you, my beautiful tree-snake!"

Sleepily, her son woke for a moment and looked up at her. He yawned, then fell back asleep.

"Do you think your little boy will be able to understand me as well?" asked the serpent.

"I do not know, Alon, but I have a strong feeling he will indeed be able to hear you as well."

The serpent smiled, then laughed in realization. "Of course! This was all meant to be! You and your son will understand me and we will all connect in a new way that has never been before! This is the sign! Our friendship is the rainbow!"

Eden, confused, simply smiled, for she was still in the afterglow of birth. Half in sleep, she accepted the serpent's words as a matter of truth, without questioning what was dream and what was waking life.

"Goodnight, my sweet Eden," said the snake as he watched mother and child drift into the world of dreams. He yawned, then drifted along with them.

Experience

*A*fter an entire year had passed, the serpent was still not allowed to see Eden, nor her infant son, Cain. Her son's name meant "Strong Tree" in Eden's language, and Alon was sure his name was in honor of him and their holy tree, and he was deeply touched. Yet, no matter how much he desperately wished to witness her child grow from boy to man, it was not meant to be.

Her husband forbade the snake's presence, even though Alon only wanted to help. Time and time again, the serpent came to meet them, but he was shooed away, and told to go back to the wild. It saddened him to his core.

"Do not worry, Alon," said Eden with a kiss to his cheek, "I am sure my husband will come around one day, and he will see you for all your wisdom and love—just as I do."

She would sneak her visits to the snake and his tree, giving him gifts of her heart, such as poems and songs. It made him feel special, but it wasn't enough.

At night, he would yearn for the sound of her voice, for Eden became more than just his friend. She was his beloved lady and his favorite person in all the world!

"Oh, Great Sky," he spoke to the clouds of midnight, "why do you torture me this way? Why can I not spend my days and my nights talking and walking with my Lovely Garden? Am I not a good snake? Do I not deserve to be happy?"

Searching for answers in the passing clouds of darkness, the serpent realized the futility of his longing, and it made him cry. "I am a fool, aren't I, Great Sky? I am in love with a human woman, though I am only a silly snake. I had hoped my dream of the rainbow would make me special, but now I fear I am too different to be a snake or a human. I am neither and both. I am *too* special!"

Feeling as though he had been stabbed by a rose's thorn, the confused serpent slid onto a large, leafy branch. His tears fell upon the tree's roots, which brought forth an extremely old magic—one that had been believed to be long since gone from the world.

Just as the serpent fell into a sad slumber, the tree became even more alive as it woke from its deep sleep.

Poor, dear, snake, it whispered into the night air. *Must you choose? Must you change?*

With those empathetic words spoken into the wind of transformative moonlight, something strange and miraculous happened to the snake.

He dreamt of change within his mind and body. Arms, legs, feet—he had them all! Walking, not slithering upon the ground, he found his way to the humans. He greeted them, and they did not hiss or jeer. Instead, they gave him clothing and food, and took him under their care.

It was a lovely dream, and he did not want to wake. If he hadn't heard Eden's voice, he never would have opened his eyes.

"But where did he come from?" she asked a woman in the cave.

"I do not know. He showed up last night... wandering without clothes, as if in a fever. He must be ill, my Queen."

"Yes..." Eden replied, "and probably from another village. We shall help him to be well again."

"But what will the king say?"

"I do not care what my husband says," Eden snapped. "This is my decision, not his."

Alon did not want to open his eyes, for he was afraid he'd gone mad within his sleep. He had no choice, however, for when he felt his beloved Eden put her hand to his forehead, he knew he must see if what he imagined was indeed true.

Slowly, he opened his eyes and saw her familiar, oval face. It was no dream! He was human! It was magic, but it was real!

The tree did this to me, thought Alon as he watched Eden repay his kindness from before by giving him water. *Somehow, it heard my wish, and it changed my form. Thank you, my friend, I will never forget what you have done for as long as I live!*

—

After a few weeks, Alon was able to sit up, drink, and eat. Eden's healer-women had been bringing him food and water, and had given him medicinal herbs. They had been nursing him in a cave near their tribe's village, but they didn't truly know what to do with the strange man they had found. With his pale, near white hair and sky-blue eyes, he looked unlike anyone they had ever seen! He was not tan and hairy like the rest of their men, and he spoke with a very strange accent; it sounded almost like he was singing.

Alon couldn't quite fathom his transformation either, nor how he could even speak their language. However, he felt it was disrespectful to question such a gift, so he merely accepted his new form with grace and love.

"Thank you for your help, but am I healed enough now to see what is outside this cave?" he asked the brown-haired woman who had brought him a basket of tasty root vegetables and deer meat.

"Yes, I think you are well enough to walk around, young stranger," she replied, blushing at his alien, yet handsome appearance, "but you will have to ask our queen if you may leave the cave."

"Will she be here today?" he asked eagerly.

"Yes," said the woman, "she will come at midday to check on you. It is Queen Eden who found you. She feels personally responsible for your well-being."

Smiling to himself, Alon was excited to see Eden once again, though he wasn't completely sure what her being a queen meant. He hoped she would recognize who he was after they spoke, and then, she would gladly welcome him into their tribe.

Unfortunately, things didn't quite happen as he expected. Though Eden seemed to somewhat recognize him, it only made her feel confused and disoriented. Alon wanted to hug her and explain he was really her beloved White Tree, but he couldn't say how it was possible, especially since he himself didn't understand. Instead, he simply said he was grateful to her for saving his life and that he wanted to repay her kindness in any way he could.

She tilted her head and looked at the familiar, pale man before her. "Thank you," she replied, "but you do not have to repay me. I am glad to help those in need. I am curious, though... about where you come from and how you came to be here. Do you come from far away? You look and sound very different."

He didn't know what to say, so he shook his head, quietly shrugging. "I don't remember," he softly replied.

"You poor man," said Eden as she helped him to his feet. "The fever must have taken your memory. But do not fear, my friend. I am sure my tribe will accept you, and we will help you begin a new life."

Smiling and following his beloved Eden into the forest clearing outside of the cave, Alon felt a cool breeze blow against his newly human skin. It felt good, and right.

"Do you remember your name?" she asked. He was nervous to tell her the name she had given him, so he hesitantly lied, telling her that he couldn't quite recall. "That's alright," said Eden with a gentle smile, "I am sure the elder-shaman of our tribe will name you. He is very good at that."

Alon nodded and happily followed behind her, feeling dazed, as if in a dream.

The tribe was curious about him, especially the children. They came forward with whispers, and some of the children even touched him to see if he was real. Alon smiled at them, and they soon scurried back to their mothers.

Eden then brought Alon to her husband, King Adam. Alon was surprised how agreeable her husband was as they shook hands in his large hut.

"Welcome, stranger," said Adam. "My wife tells me how you fell in the forest to a terrible fever and that you can no longer remember even your own name. What an ordeal you must have been through. Please, relax and drink some wine."

"Thank you," replied Alon.

"You are most welcome in our tribe," said Adam, "for as long as you wish to stay."

He never wanted to even look upon my face when I was a serpent, thought Alon. *But that's alright. I'm just glad he's friendly with me now.*

They talked about many things: the tribe, their hunting and gathering customs, even Adam's name and how it meant "Sacred Soil." Adam explained how his mother was a healer, and his father was the elder-shaman of the tribe. Eden was his cousin on his mother's side, and their union had been arranged since they were young children.

"Of course, I took one look at my beautiful cousin," said Adam with a kiss to his wife's hand, "and I knew my parents had chosen wisely."

Alon was jealous, but he kept his envy at bay. *He is her husband, after all,* he told himself as he drank his cup of wine and nodded with a smile.

"Is your father still the shaman?" asked Alon.

"Sadly, he is rather old now," replied Adam, "and he is in the process of searching for an apprentice to take his place. Would you like to meet my father? I have a feeling he'd be very interested in helping you to remember yourself."

"That is a wonderful idea, my king!" said Eden. "I am certain he can help our guest remember through use of dream questing!"

"Absolutely," replied Adam. "I will go to him right now and arrange a meeting before the tribe meets for dinner. Stay here. I'll be back in a moment."

"You are very kind, my king, thank you," said Alon.

The king got up and left Eden and Alon alone in the hut. She smiled nervously, making Alon do the same. There was a tension—an unspoken connection that could not be acted upon.

After a few minutes, the curly-haired woman who had healed him came in to break the silence. "My queen," she said.

"Yes, Bala?"

"Cain is crying. I think he may need you to feed him."

"Oh, please bring him to me," replied Eden.

Bala then brought Eden's son to her bosom, and Alon watched in awe as she fed her hungry son.

"So beautiful," said Alon, unable to keep his feelings to himself.

Eden bashfully smiled and said, "Thank you, my friend. I hope that Adam's father, our elder-shaman, can sense your name soon, so that I may address you properly. Somehow, I feel as though I've known you for a long time, yet I know we've not met before the day I found you in the forest."

Alon was at a loss for words. All he could do was stare at Eden's soft breast and her suckling son, wishing with all his heart that he was a part of their family.

"Good news!" said Adam, startling Alon. "My father will see you after dinner. He even said that the spirits told him about you already, and he feels he can help you to remember."

Alon nodded and thanked his king, though inside, he was anything but happy. The serpent inside him was coiling up in pain, wishing he could be fully human with Eden and her baby. He wished he could tell her how he transformed to be with her, but he knew she'd never believe such magic existed. He wasn't even sure if he believed it anymore.

Am I crazy? Was I ever a snake in the forest or did I dream it when I fell into the fever? I can no longer tell what is truth. Is this what it is to be human? So much pain... so much confusion.

Alon almost began to cry, but he did not want Eden, nor her husband, to see him in tears.

Holding his emotions inside, Alon followed the king and queen as they led him into the tribe's eating area. Eden gave her son to Bala to take care of while she sat with her husband as they were served various meats and vegetables. Alon was given a stone-carved seat near them and given the same offering of food.

Everyone seemed cheerful and secure in their tribe. All loved their king and queen, and they loved their "Heavenly Father," as they called their sky spirit. Alon had always loved the sky and found it easy to join their prayer to the mysterious father they all thanked for their food and hearth.

After dinner, there was a drum ritual where a few of the hunters recited poems about their great hunting adventures. Alon was captivated! Then, there was dancing, singing, and smoking.

While enjoying the rituals of the tribe, Alon was tapped on the shoulder by the elder-shaman. "Come with me, Serpent," said the old man with long, gray hair.

Alon was utterly shocked and thought, *How does he know my true nature? How can he possibly see my soul?*

The elder-shaman grinned and said, "Let's go now... into my hut, and we will drink the milk of the sky. You will soon remember your true self."

Alon was terrified, but he did as the old man said and followed him into his hut. It was filled with objects of stone and clay. On the objects were paintings and words: holy words with sacred meanings.

The elder-shaman picked up a large clay cup and said, "This represents your heart, and the milk I am about to pour into it symbolizes your spirit. When your heart is filled with your spirit, you will remember the truth of your soul."

Alon gulped his nerves down along with the strange, bitter tasting milk that the elder-shaman gave him. After a few seconds, his mind spun, and everything in the hut went hazy.

"Do you see your true self?" asked the old man.

"No... wait... yes," whispered Alon.

"What do you see? Do you see your serpentine spirit?"

"Yes... but it is more," Alon replied in a hushed, low voice. "He... I was... more."

"More? What do you see?"

Alon sat down on the elder-shaman's furry rug and gathered his image in his mind. It was his old body that he saw, but his skin was silky smooth and reflecting the sun's light. In his vision, it started to rain. The droplets of water fell on the pale snake's skin and created a glow in the sun.

"It's me, but... his skin is so shiny... so beautiful. I never saw myself like that before."

"Yes..." said the elder-shaman, "that is your true self. You are protected by the serpent spirit, and he is giving you a vision of the truth."

"The truth?" asked Alon. "The truth of what?"

"The truth of your path and why you are here!"

Alon shook his head slowly, trying his best to understand what he saw and what the old man was telling him. Then, he saw the snake smile at the sun, and his near translucent skin turned into a multicolored pattern. It meant something important, but Alon couldn't find its meaning.

"Why am I here?" Alon said, turning to the elder-shaman with tears forming in his eyes.

The old man gave Alon a sympathetic smile and said, "Only you can find that answer, my friend. But you have a strong spirit guardian, and its magic surrounds you. I have a feeling you will find the answers you seek... and very soon."

Alon hoped the elder-shaman was right as he fell into a deep, vision-filled sleep.

The animals were all there in the great plains of the sun. Even the giant Elephant king was there with his enormous tusks pointing up toward the sky. It was a gathering unlike any of the past!

"Have you all come to hear my testimony?" asked the serpent.

The animals all replied with their unique voices. Unfortunately, Alon couldn't understand what they were saying. The lion roared, and the elephants trumpeted. The monkeys screamed, and the birds sang. It was all a mysterious, lost language to him now, and he stood in the center of the animals, confused.

What was I here to tell them? he wondered. *It was something about the rainbow, but... I don't exactly remember.*

Then, the clouds parted, and the serpent stood up like a man. He extended his arms above him and reached for the sky. "Father?" he addressed the sky. "Is this what you wanted? Should I be a man now? Please tell me! I am your faithful messenger, and I will spread your glory, if that is my path. But please, Father, tell me what it is that you wish me to do and say!"

The sky grumbled and the clouds went dark. Lightning shot across the sky as Alon got his answer in the form of thunder and rain.

No... he must not want me to be a man, thought Alon. *But why? Can I not enjoy what others enjoy? Why was I given the hunger and the yearning if I cannot love and express like the others can?*

"Father!" he shouted into the stormy sky. "Don't you see that I am no longer an animal? I cannot even speak or hear their languages any longer. I am not an animal, yet I am not a man. What am I? Am I a snake or a human? Father? Do you hear me? Do you care?"

The sky changed yet again, and Alon saw everything in fast motion. The earth itself grew and died, and grew again. Trees and flowers gave way to floods and fires, then grew back. Time itself flew as fast as a rushing river, and Alon saw all of Creation's inescapable, endless cycle of rebirth. Fragile and delicate, yet unending and invincible, the earth displayed its power and revealed the sky's ultimate answer: evolve.

Time regained its regular speed as Alon woke to the sound of birds chirping. He was still in the elder-shaman's hut, though he could have sworn he had travelled far, far away.

Grinning with a few missing molars, the old shaman handed Alon a cup of tea. "Drink," he said as Alon took the tea, "it will help you adjust back to this realm of reality."

Sipping the hot tea, Alon asked, "Is there another realm?"

"There are many," replied the elder-shaman with a devious grin. Alon was confused, but drank and felt his mind re-focusing on what he knew to be true. He knew he was a man and that he was in a tribe that felt like home. He couldn't quite remember any specifics about his past, but he remembered he was part of a big family—a giant tribe filled with many diverse and interesting people.

"Is it possible that I am from a large tribe from the East?" Alon asked the elder shaman.

"Yes, it is possible," he replied, "but only you can know for sure. Did the sky-milk give you a vision?"

Alon nodded and said, "By the spirits, it definitely did!"

"Well? What did it show you?"

Alon hesitated at first, then he slowly unravelled his dream to the elder-shaman.

Amazed, the old man rubbed his head and said, "So you have been chosen to wear the eyes of the sky."

"What?" asked Alon.

"I had known your soul wore the sign of the serpent, but I had no idea you had been chosen to see with The Father's own eyes! Joyous day! I have finally found my apprentice!"

"But I—"

"No, you cannot refuse," said the elated old man. "It has already been decided! You, my serpent friend, are now the tribe's new shaman-to-be!"

Surprised, yet honored, Alon smiled as the old man hugged him. Afterward, the elder-shaman revealed his name to be Adaman. It soon became obvious to Alon that the elder-shaman had hoped his own son would become a shaman as well, though his wish had not been fulfilled.

Unfortunately, Adam's leadership only extended as far as keeping the order of the tribe. "His prowess with pleasing his people is impressive," said Adaman, "but my son has never been skilled with seeing the spirit of the world. It was just not his path, I suppose. But you can be his eyes! You were meant to be part of this tribe, and you will help us find a new connection to The Father."

Alon wasn't so sure if that was indeed his purpose, but he wanted very much to belong in the tribe and to become the elder-shaman's apprentice. Most of all, he hoped Eden would approve and be pleased.

That night, the elder-shaman announced his choice for apprentice to the tribe. He even told them that the Sky Father himself had named his apprentice Alon because, out of all creation's animals, the pale serpent of the trees was the most aware of the world.

The tribe had given up on him choosing anyone, so they were shocked, though happy. Eden, however, was a little more than disturbed by the name given to the pale stranger. It unnerved her, and yet, she welcomed him warmly.

"It is a new dawn!" decreed Adam as he patted Alon's back. Alon worried that the king might feel as if his birthright had been stolen, but Adam seemed to be nothing but supportive and full of smiles. Eden too appeared joyful and serene. All was good. All was right.

Evolve, thought Alon. *That is exactly what I will do, and I will bring harmony to my tribe. I promise you, Sky Father, with all my heart.*

In the coming passings of the moon, everyone got used to Alon and treated him, and his pale skin, as though he had always been there. His rightful place had been established, and no one doubted him.

One brisk autumn night, the elder-shaman died peacefully in his bed, having taught Alon everything he could about seeing the spirits, and communicating with them.

Then, the king and queen, and the entire tribe, held a bonfire in his honor. The king scattered his father's ashes into the soil where his mother's ashes already lay. It was a subtle, beautiful ritual that touched Alon's soul. It was also his first time acting as shaman. He had given a speech about Adaman, which made more than a few tear up with sadness and joy. Alon also told of how great of a father the elder-shaman had been and how he had always seen spirits, even as a boy.

In Alon's short time with Adaman, he had grown quite close to his teacher, and it hurt him to speak as if Adaman was gone.

Alon knew better though, for he was wise to the fact that no one ever truly died. "They only leave this realm that we see with our eyes," he told his tribe. "Our bodies may dissolve into dust, but our spirits never die, and our souls continue into the unseen spirit realm. I know for certain we will see our great elder-shaman again, especially in dreams, which tell us truths hidden within the illusion."

Adam half-smiled through his tears and whispered to his wife, "He reminds me of my father... when he was younger—when I was a boy."

"Yes, your father chose well," replied Eden as she held her husband's hand. She loved Adam, but never quite the way he loved her. He gave her warmth and attention, but he had a hard time going deep into her soul, and the same distance he kept with spirits, he also kept with love making.

He meant well, and was handsome with golden-brown waves of hair, blue-gray eyes, and angular jaw, but she did not feel passionately for him. Although she yearned to love him with all her soul, she just couldn't do it.

In return, Adam loved his wife with every fiber of his being, though he didn't know how to please her. He often gave her smooth stones and flowers in effort to match her outer beauty, and he often told her how lovely she was, but nothing he said or did seemed to truly impress his beloved Eden.

She was never cruel, however. In fact, she was always loving and good to him, but there was still something missing, though he couldn't place what it was. There seemed to be lacking a certain kind of fire between them, but he didn't know why.

Growing up, Adam's mother told him to be patient with women, especially with his precocious cousin. Adam knew that his mother was right, so he waited until Eden seemed open to his proposal before bedding her.

Eden was a healer, born of a healer and a star-seer, therefore Adam was aware of how smart his betrothed was before they wed. He was patient like his mother told him to be, and yet, even in their most heated mating, something was missing. Afterward, Adam always felt the need to go into the night and look at the stars. Eden was left to fall asleep alone.

Their marital problems were unknown to Alon, though he could sense their tension. He wanted to help them, but knew not how. Adam usually kept such problems to himself, and Alon's hidden feelings for Eden would not allow him to think objectively.

Months went by and Alon gave advice, had visions, and spoke to departed loved ones. The king often asked Alon to interpret his dreams as well. Alon saw the truth of the hidden symbols quickly; it came easily to him. It made the king happy, and they soon became friends.

Eden was also drawn to Alon's spiritually wise nature. Truthfully, she was attracted to Alon in ways she wished she wasn't, but she held her feelings back, deep within her breast.

However, she couldn't stop herself from visiting his hut, especially when Cain began having nightmares. She didn't know why a small child would have such unexplainable fears, and she hoped Alon would have an answer.

"Monsters," she told him. "He usually dreams about monsters."

"What do they look like?" he asked her as he gave her a cup of calming, herbal tea.

"I'm not sure. He has only just learned to speak. He says they're big and scary. That's all I know."

Alon assured her that her son's nightmares would eventually stop, but until then, he gave her a bag of the calming tea she was drinking and told her to give it to her son.

"Thank you, Shaman," she said as she turned to leave. Just as she was about to exit his hut, something compelled her to stay. "Alon?" she said, turning to face him.

"Yes?"

"Do you think I'm a good mother?"

Astonished by the question, he said, "What? Of course, my queen! You are a very good mother. Why would you ask me that?"

"I am worried for my son. I just hope that I didn't do anything to bring these nightmares to him."

"No, my queen, of course you didn't. I am sure he just—"

"I need to confess something," she interrupted.

"Alright," said Alon as he offered her a fur-covered chair made of stone.

She nervously sat down, then said, "When I was pregnant with Cain, I was scared about giving birth, about my marriage, and so many things. I was young, and I still dreamt of being free. I wanted to be a healer... like my mother was.

However, my new husband didn't want me to spend energy helping others, so I stopped my studies and kept my dreams to myself. I've always been spiritually inclined as well, Alon, and I even wrote songs for the rituals, but Adam didn't want me to disturb the tribe with the notion of a queen who can do such things. I had to keep it in... and I was not happy."

"I see," said Alon, nodding sadly.

"So I went to the old tree in the forest... near the great plains where the animals roam. I know it was dangerous, but I felt the need to go there deep in my soul. I can't explain it, but I had to be there for Cain's birth. I wanted to feel the Sky Father's warmth, and that was where I felt him most."

"Yes," said Alon, "you were right, my queen. That is where the sky feels strongest."

"Please, you may call me Eden. We are friends, are we not?"

"Yes, we are," replied Alon with a bashful smile.

Eden tried not to look at his smile, for it was warm and inviting. Instead, she looked down and let her mind be taken by fears. "Oh, my friend... I hope I am not being punished now for my indiscretion. You see, when I got to the tree, I met a beautiful white snake, and his presence somehow comforted me. I was able to give birth without fear."

"That sounds like it was a blessing, not a punishment," said Alon, his own memory beginning to rustle inside his brain. *Was I that white snake? I can't imagine how that could be, but somehow, her story is so familiar.*

"I didn't think it was wrong, so I visited the snake several times afterward. I gave him gifts for helping me. I even sang to him and loved him through my words. I even gave him a name... Your name."

"My name?" asked Alon nervously.

"Yes, strange, I know. It was as if he was your guardian spirit before you came here. I loved him very much, but one day, he completely disappeared. I worry it was my fault that he left. I must have offended him somehow, and I fear that I upset the great Sky Father... and now my son is suffering because of my foolishness."

Bursting into tears, she held her face and cried.

"No, Eden..." he softly spoke. "You are not to blame."

Alon was afraid to touch her, for fear his aching heart might love her too intensely, but he knew she needed his warmth. Unable to stop himself, he wrapped his arms around her shoulders and held her close. She cried into his arms, and it felt like home... to both of them.

Slowly, she looked up and their eyes met. She saw his sky-blue eyes and became lost in them. He too felt caught in her deep-green gaze. As if in a spell, they were pulled to each other until their lips touched. Unable to pull away, they kissed, softly at first, and then more and more passionately.

The world spun and time sped, much like in his first vision, and they found themselves needing each other in a sensually explosive, almost primal way.

"Take me!" she gasped as she removed her green dress.

He could not refuse. Their clothing came off as if it was the most painful burden to wear them, and soon they were lying in his white fur-bed.

On top of his beloved Eden, he saw the universe in her eyes. Deep inside her and moving in time with her breathing, he felt his own sacred truth: evolve... but only with her! "Always with you... only with you... forever," he whispered, lost inside her.

She whimpered and arched her back as they became one.

"I love you," he said looking in her eyes, through to her very soul.

She wanted to say it in return, but was frightened. Instead, she smiled and held him in her arms. They knew they only had a brief time together, but it felt as if time stood still, and for a moment, they were purely happy.

Knowledge

Cain was a bright boy—so much that his parents often wondered if he was almost too smart for his own good. He had grown up well, however, and just as Alon had predicted, the nightmares eventually stopped. They were soon replaced with wild dreams where he adventured through the stars and met the monsters he once feared. Alon had helped him turn his mind's monsters into beings whom he only needed to know well enough to speak with, as if they were his close friends.

Cain looked up to Alon, his teacher and friend, and he loved him like a second father. However, the jealousy he felt about his little brother was a problem.

Abel was too much like their shaman—in appearance and in demeanor. Even King Adam, Cain's father, seemed unnerved at times by their similarity. Nothing was ever said aloud, but Cain had a sneaking suspicion that Abel was not really his father's son. He never said a word, however, for fear it might break up the tribe, which was something Cain was not willing to risk.

Cain loved his little brother, but they were very different from each other. Cain had dark hair with dark blue eyes and was brash and bold, always speaking his mind and questing after the newest discovery without fear. Abel was questing too, in his own way, but he was quiet and soft-spoken with pale skin, light hair and sky-blue eyes.

Cain often wanted to explore the hidden caves and valleys around their tribe, but Abel didn't want to disobey his father who prohibited such distant areas.

"They could be dangerous!" Abel protested.

"Yes, but that's what makes it an adventure!" Cain replied with a wild grin.

Once again, Abel refused to go with him and said, "I'm going to Shaman Alon, and I'll tell him you're not coming to his class again."

"Go ahead," Cain said with a shrug, "he won't care. You're his favorite student anyway."

"That's not true. He loves you!" argued Abel. "He always talks about how smart you are... even if you're hot-headed and impatient too."

Cain cracked his neck, trying his best to ignore the jab by his little brother. *He doesn't even know he does it,* thought Cain. *It must be because he's so different looking and doesn't know why. Maybe he's jealous of me in return? I don't know why he would be, but Alon says we must always try to see other people's points of view and empathize.*

He was right. Abel envied his brother very much. In Abel's mind, Cain was perfect: dashingly handsome, heroic, fun, and magnanimous. Everyone adored him, and in comparison, Abel felt like a shadow or an afterthought. He couldn't see his own beauty or intelligence; he only saw his strangeness and shyness.

Both brothers had no idea of their true worth. It was a problem that Alon was well aware of, though he wasn't sure how to guide them without overstepping his bounds.

He had promised his beloved Eden he would never speak about or act upon their brief, yet passionate mating. It nearly destroyed him to keep that promise, but he loved her beyond measure, so he kept silent.

He knew she had valid reasons for their distance; if Adam found out about their lovemaking, it could result in the fall of the tribe. Adam was their leader, and even though he was strong and good, he was also a sensitive, emotional man. Eden feared the truth would rip his heart apart, and she couldn't do that to him, nor to her family.

So Alon kept his needs deep inside the back of his heart while he swallowed his pride. He was almost completely sure that Abel was of his own flesh and blood, but he swallowed that as well. *For Eden,* he told himself, *I must not let my ego win. I must learn to let go.*

He allowed himself to love her in secret though. No one could take that from him. He also loved her children—both of them equally. He even loved Adam. They were all his soul's family, and he wanted nothing more than to protect and guide them.

Abel, however, was special. Even his name, which meant "Breath of the Sky," was from a poem Eden had once secretly written for her beloved serpent. Alon easily saw himself in Abel, and it was nearly impossible for him to ignore their close bond.

He is my son... I know it in my heart, thought Alon as he helped Abel with his stone-writing. There was nothing he could say or do, but he yearned to claim the boy as his own.

Smiling at his teacher, Abel loved to learn and impress. "Is the symbol for 'dream' like this?" asked Abel as he showed Alon the painted stone he had just completed.

"Yes! Well done, Abel!"

Beaming with pride, Abel set his stone in the corner and said, "Will I be able to carve it tomorrow?"

"Yes," said Alon, "once it dries, you may shape it with the sander."

Alon loved his studious boy, and Abel loved his teacher just as much. Their bond was undeniable.

Cain tried to ignore their bond as he focused instead on making his own markings and symbols in caves that had yet to be discovered. Dipping his forefinger into the black goo with only firelight to guide him, he feverishly painted on the wall. He knew his artwork would impress Shaman Alon, as well as his mother and father.

He even hoped to gain the attention of the entire tribe, especially the pretty brown-haired daughter of his mother's midwife, Bala. Her name was Hana, and she was actually his second cousin, but he didn't mind. He liked that she was already family. Besides, most of the tribe were related—some more closely than others.

Hana seemed to like Cain, as she was always smiling at him when he walked past her, but he had to be sure before asking for her hand in marriage. They were young yet too. He knew he had time.

Stroke after stroke with his fingers, Cain found himself creating a giant buffalo. He was still not allowed to hunt yet, for he was a few months shy of manhood, but he had seen it from afar. Without his father knowing, Cain had watched the swift capturing, and then killing, of the giant beast. It was horrific, yet fascinating!

Telling the story of the hunt with his fingers, Cain kept going until he broke a sweat. Stepping back to view his painting, he saw the hunters with their spears, and his own father at the front. They were taking down the mighty buffalo, and Cain felt he had captured the action perfectly!

Just wait until Father sees this! thought Cain. *He'll cry and crush me with a proud embrace!*

Adam never crushed anyone with emotional embraces; it wasn't his nature, but Cain hoped to change his father, no matter what it took.

After spending far too long in the cave, Cain realized the sun had fallen, and the moon was now shining brightly. Knowing he'd be in trouble, he rushed home, hoping they wouldn't notice his absence.

"Where were you?!" shouted Adam. Cain had no answer except, "I... I'm sorry, Father."

"Don't you know how worried your mother and I have been?" scolded Adam.

Cain was silent, unable to explain about his cave paintings. He was too afraid his father wouldn't approve.

Walking up to Cain's side, Alon put his hand on Cain's shoulder and said, "I'm sorry, my king, but he was running an errand for me."

Cain looked up at his teacher, confused.

"You see," Alon continued, "I needed more milky stems for my vision questing, and your dutiful elder-son was willing to help me pick them. I'm afraid it's a tedious task, and he probably lost track of time. It won't happen again. Will it, Prince Cain?"

Cain shook his head, grateful for his teacher's lie, and said, "No, it won't. I promise."

"Fine," said Adam, "but if you are going to help the shaman again, please tell us first so we can find you, if needs be, and so we won't have to worry."

Letting out a frustrated exhale, Adam motioned for Cain to sit by his side. It was the middle of dinner, and everyone had stopped eating. Once the king and queen returned to eating, the rest of the tribe resumed as well.

Alon then sat down next to Eden and drank some wine.

"Thank you," she whispered to him with a knowing smile. He nodded in return and winked. Their language was always unsaid, but very strong. They almost spoke in their minds, and both Cain and Adam were well aware of the strong bond between them.

At that moment, however, Cain wasn't bothered about his mother's connection with his teacher. He was more concerned with what Hana thought about him being late. She had looked at him with a peculiar glance, and he wasn't sure if she was interested in him or if she just didn't approve. She was hard to read, unlike his mother.

Eden had always doted on Cain, and he loved her deeply, but he also loved his emotionally distant, demanding father. He deeply cared for his teacher too. It was impossible for him to take sides.

Looking over at Abel, he wished he was more oblivious, like his younger brother. Abel was gnawing on a bone, and Cain thought he seemed happily unaware of everything going on around them.

He was wrong, however, for Abel had a special ability—one he didn't like to talk about, even with their shaman. Ever since he had been old enough to walk, Abel could hear things: sounds... whispers... feelings. Sometimes he heard people's thoughts, and it frightened him. Even more frightening was when he saw spirits, though he knew they meant no harm. Usually, they were just lost and needed help finding their way.

These gifts were Abel's secret. He hadn't told Cain, nor his mother and father. The only person who knew of Abel's spiritual talents was Alon, though he had promised to keep it quiet.

Abel was embarrassed and confused about why he would be able to hear and see such incredible things. Alon knew why, however, and it made him proud.

Despite his gifts, Abel wasn't quite ready to become his teacher's apprentice, and Alon realized he would have to wait and be patient. Besides, he was certain Abel would eventually come to him, wishing to learn everything Alon had to offer. In the meantime, he was happy to teach both sons the basics of reading and writing symbols, as well as how to collect herbs and decipher their uses.

Alon hadn't been completely fibbing when he said he'd given Cain the task of finding the milk-stems. He had, although Cain had forgotten the task completely. Alon knew he'd have to talk to him about his cave outings, especially if he was out after dark.

After dinner, Alon brought Cain outside to speak with him alone.

"But I'm almost a man!" said Cain, defending himself. "I should be trusted enough that I can go into the forest by myself."

"Don't be so hasty to grow up," Alon calmly replied. "Becoming an adult isn't as rewarding as it may seem."

"What does that mean?" asked Cain, squinting his dark-blue eyes.

"It means that you are still a young man, and you need to do as your father says."

"Oh right, as if you do what he says," said Cain, sarcasm dripping off his words.

Alon puckered his lips and furrowed his brow. He didn't like Cain's tone one bit.

"As brave and smart as you are, my prince," he stoically replied, "you are still under your father's care, and your mother worries for you a great deal. When you leave and do not tell anyone where you're going, it does nothing but cause her grief. Is that what you want?"

"No..." Cain muttered under his breath.

"Then, please, from now on, do as your father and I ask. Tell us where you are going, and do not stay after dark."

"He wouldn't understand," said Cain, angrily pouting. "He wouldn't let me do it if I told him."

"What is it you're doing?" asked Alon, curious.

"I am... painting."

A great smile came over Alon's face. "You are? How wonderful! May I see it?"

Cain broke a smile, but was embarrassed. "I don't know..." he replied shyly, "it's still not finished, and it's dark now, so you probably wouldn't be able to see it very well."

"I am sure I will love it!" said Alon. "Why don't you take me to see it first thing in the morning?"

Cain was scared, but agreed. He yearned to show his paintings to someone, and he trusted Alon's opinion. Alon himself was an excellent symbol maker and painter of stones.

By the next morning, shaman and elder-prince went to the forest's cave where he'd been painting his elaborate hunting scene. Little did they know they were secretly being followed by an inquisitive mind.

When Alon saw Cain's intricate artwork, he gasped with joy. "This is glorious!" he exclaimed. "You must show the tribe!"

"Oh… I don't know about that," replied Cain nervously. "I don't think they'd react like you. They might even laugh."

Alon smirked and said, "Your fears are unfounded. Trust me, they will love it… especially your father."

"No, he won't," Cain sadly replied. "He will say I shouldn't have even come here. He probably won't even see that I depicted his likeness."

Alon looked closer at the painting and said, "Oh, yes! I see the king leading the hunt. How wonderful. You've even painted the buffalo's spirit! It's majestic, my boy. You really should be proud of your work."

Cain smiled, beginning to let Alon's words into his heart.

Just then, prying sky-blue eyes could take no more as Abel rushed inside to see what their teacher had been gushing about. Taking a good look at the painting, Abel gasped and said, "So this is what you've been doing in here, brother! It's amazing!"

Abel then gave Cain a warm embrace. The two brothers talked and laughed as the three of them had a lunch of apples and nuts. All was good. All was right.

—

Hana liked Cain's bravery with a spear and his dashing confidence. She also liked his artwork and his humor. He was everything a young woman could want.

Unfortunately, she was in love with his younger brother. With his radiant sky-blue eyes, his warm smile and poetic words, Abel had quickly won her heart, and she couldn't quell her desire. He hadn't even pursued her the way Cain had, and yet, she was lost in love for the shaman-in-training.

Both boys had grown into handsome, intelligent young men, but if she had to choose, she couldn't help loving Abel with all her soul – if only he'd notice!

Unfortunately, Abel had no idea how Hana felt. He spent most of his time studying symbols and having visions, so he wasn't aware of how she looked at him with attentive eyes or how she would smile when he walked past. Also, he had gotten used to tuning out other people's thoughts so he could concentrate on his own. It was a technique Alon had shown him, and it worked. Unfortunately, it worked a little too well at times, making him oblivious to Hana's affection.

Even still, she adored him. It was so apparent, in fact, that Cain had more than noticed. He didn't understand why she would even want his younger brother and not him. He accepted that his little brother was handsome and kind, but he also thought Abel was a little inept and clueless. "Off in the clouds" was what Adam used to say about Abel, and Cain agreed.

In contrast, Eden often stood up for her younger son. She reminded her husband and elder son that Abel was a very smart shaman-in-training, and if he had to be in the clouds to speak with the spirits, then that was part of his soul's path.

It bothered her greatly that Adam emotionally distanced from, not only Abel, but Cain as well. Her husband seemed to be distancing from everyone as he got older, including her.

"What is wrong, my great king?" she asked him as they lay down to sleep in their fur bed. He didn't answer; he only shook his head and sighed. "You seem so worried all the time... so agitated. Is there anything I can do?"

"No," he mumbled as he shut his eyes to sleep.

She wished she had the gift of hearing thoughts – the way Abel had been gifted as a child. He didn't seem to enjoy his gift, however, and now, he had pulled away from it. *Everyone is pulling away from their true selves,* she thought. She didn't like that idea. It felt wrong.

There was nothing she could do to help though. Everyone seemed out of her reach… except for Alon. He was always responsive and understanding. Any time she needed his advice or his attention, he was there. She tried to keep her feelings for him unnoticeable, but the more Adam distanced, the more she went to Alon for comfort.

Her secret desire for him had not diminished through the years, and she knew he felt the same. Though they kept their love silent and had not been physically close since their one night fifteen years prior, their intimate glances said it all.

Adam had never caught his wife in the act of infidelity, but he suspected it nonetheless. He had been watching their interactions together for many years, and he was certain that Alon had made love to his wife at least once, if not more. The very thought drove him to the brink of rage, and yet, for the love of his children and his tribe, he kept his anger cool. He had once loved Alon like a brother, but now… he could no longer feel the same.

Alon sensed how Adam felt, but he couldn't even broach the subject, for fear the conversation would escalate into something irreversibly dark. Alon couldn't lie. If Adam questioned his feelings for Eden, he was sure his answer would instigate a fight, and that was something he refused to let happen.

—

Time went by, and the tribe watched as the princes grew into men with drive and purpose. Cain was a great hunter, painter, and singer while Abel was a vision-questing storyteller. Together, they gave the tribe hope and strength. Despite their differences, the two brothers had become close friends as they depended on each other for guidance, and it made their parents, and their shaman, proud.

One day, Cain officially asked Hana to be his wife, and she consented. It was a joyous day full of feasting and family. However, all but Hana felt exuberant. Hana was scared, though she knew it was a great honor to become the next queen. She decided to ask Queen Eden what to do.

"Just love him," Eden simply stated. "That is all you can do in marriage, and hope for the best."

It wasn't quite the words Hana was looking for. Confused and needing fresh air from all the merrymaking, Hana sneaked away from the party, hoping she could clear her mind while taking a nice walk in the forest.

She loved the time between day and night, when the drowsy sun slipped into its night-time slumber. She sighed as she strolled through the outskirts of the tribe.

She soon came upon her favorite tree, the great apple tree of time. She stroked its jagged, old, and very thick trunk. She had been picking apples with her family since she could remember, and it always gave them a sense of oneness with the bounty of the earth.

"Oh, great apple tree," she sighed, "what should I do? Am I ready to be queen? Is this the right path for me? Should I marry Cain and forget my true feelings? Will that bring everyone happiness?"

Waiting for an answer or a sign, she closed her eyes and listened to the sound of the tree branches swaying in the wind.

Forgetting time itself, she didn't expect an actual voice to say, "You should do what your heart feels is right."

Stunned, she opened her green eyes and saw her beloved young man with golden hair. The voice belonged to Abel, and he was leaning against the apple tree with his arms folded. He had followed her, concerned about her well-being.

She couldn't help but smile, though she tried to suppress her giddiness. "Did you follow me?" she asked, blushing.

"I was worried, and so was Cain. You just disappeared... from your own engagement party. That is not what a future princess should do, Hana."

"Don't scold me, Apprentice Shaman," she teased. "I am your senior, and I will be your queen someday."

Abel smiled, amused at her playful arrogance. "You will make a fine queen, Hana," he replied, "but only if you can obey your husband."

She frowned and said, "Cain cannot control me."

"No... he can't," said Abel, "but I know my brother. He is old-fashioned, much like our father is. It's not really his fault... but you need to tell him when you go take walks like this or he, and everyone, will worry."

"He used to go off into the forest when he was younger!" she argued. "I remember it well. It's what I liked about him most, I think."

Abel nodded and replied, "I know... but he is different now. He will be king, and that is a responsibility you will have to have on your shoulders as well... for the sake of the tribe."

"It's not fair," she pouted. "Why do we get assigned these roles? How did you escape it, Abel? Is it all just luck?"

He shook his head and smirked. "You think I've escaped responsibility?" he replied. "That is absolutely not true. I am Shaman Alon's apprentice, and I help him to understand everyone's fears and dreams – even the king's. I have to be there for the whole tribe, no matter when and how. It is not something easy, Hana."

"No, I didn't mean that you don't have duties," she said, leaning against the tree. "I just meant that you get to go where you want. How many times have I seen you here at the apple tree while you're thinking to yourself or day-dreaming? You have much more freedom than the rest of us because everyone knows you will be shaman someday and that you need to be close to nature. But... it is not that way for me, even though I love nature like she were my own mother! I yearn to be close to her bosom so that I can be free, yet I am not allowed freedom. I am my father's daughter, and now I will be Cain's bride. I hate this! It's all too much constriction!"

He understood her feelings, but didn't know what to say. Women had their place in their tribe once they became wives. It was tradition to treat them almost like objects, and even though he disagreed with it, there was nothing he could do except to slowly change Cain's mind.

He was working on his brother's outlook, but he knew it would take time. Abel wanted to explain that to Hana, but he didn't think it was what she wanted to hear. He was also slightly unnerved that she had watched him by the apple tree. In his suppressed empathic ability, he sensed the reason why she had watched him, but he was afraid to ask.

"Abel?" she interrupted his thoughts.

"Yes, Hana?"

Turning to face him in the glow of sunset with her soft, brown hair blowing in the breeze, Hana blinked at him and said, "Do you think I'm beautiful?"

Surprised at her question, Abel quickly replied, "Of course I do. Why do you ask?"

She shook her head and smiled. "Do you really not know?" she asked as she twirled the bottom of her hair. Looking up at him as if he were the warmth of the sun itself, she lifted her chin to his. She was caught in his spell and forgot all about her engagement. All that mattered was her heart beating and Abel's sky-blue eyes.

He never imagined he'd kiss any woman, let alone his brother's betrothed, but it happened nonetheless. Under the setting sun, Hana's trembling lips touched his, and for a few moments, their spirits joined together.

Lost in sensual transgression, they didn't notice the apple falling to the ground. Its seeds were ready to give its nourishment, and in turn, the nearby hummingbird was more than ready to take its fill of the apple.

Love is truth, thought Alon as he secretly watched the young lovers under the tree. *There is no hiding from it.* He was saddened, and yet, warmed by the sight of his son mating for the first time. It was too much of a repeat of his own past, however, and he didn't want his beloved Abel to hurt the way he had.

Walking away from the passionate young lovers as they hungrily disrobed, Alon left to meditate by his own tree – the White Tree – where he had often dreamed of having once been a wise, white serpent.

"What is right, Father?" he asked the sky. "What is wrong? What is truth and what is moral? Does there always have to be a choice and a sacrifice?"

As usual, the sky didn't give him a direct answer. All he could do was meditate and pray, hoping the answers would reveal themselves in the shapes of clouds or in the sounds of animals. *Animals...* thought Alon, *how I wish I could be like them: simple, honest... free.*

Drifting into the dream world, Alon saw his beloved Eden coming to him while he lay under their holy tree. "My sweet serpent," she cooed at him.

Kissing her mouth, his tongue tasted her very soul. Longing became the joining of their bodies, and their union soon became children. As if she had become a great flood, Alon saw Eden give birth to hundreds of babies! They were everywhere in a gushing river of blood, water, and time. It was too much to take into his mind, and he felt he might drown at the very thought!

Waking up abruptly, Alon immediately felt something had gone wrong. He hadn't slept long, but he was sure The Sky had told him something, though he wasn't certain about its meaning. All he knew was that his gut was wrenching, and the sky was turning dark.

Dusk was falling fast as Cain screamed, "How dare you?!"

"I'm sorry, brother!" replied Abel, husky-voiced from tears.

Cain shook his head and yelled, "No! I was talking to you... you WHORE! Answer me!"

Hana was shaking all over. Half-dressed and crying, she couldn't speak for fear of what Cain might say or do. She knew he was fierce in battle, but she had never seen him so menacing. It terrified her.

"Brother... please," Abel said in a calm, tender voice, "it wasn't her fault. It just happened. I'm so sorry."

Cain turned his wild-eyed, yet stony face to Abel. Breathing hard, Cain went silent for a few seconds, and Abel wondered if his brother was beginning to calm down.

Unfortunately, Cain was on the brink of madness. He had loved Hana since childhood and was going to marry her, and no one else. It was *his* right – *his* fate.

Suddenly pushing Abel hard against the apple tree, Cain growled, "You will never call me brother again! EVER!"

"Leave him alone!" yelped Hana.

Cain ignored her and grabbed Abel's throat. "You think I didn't know how you secretly wanted her? You think I've been stupid? I may not have visions like you, but I know just as much! You've wanted her all along, you thief! Admit it!"

Of course, with Cain's right hand on his throat, Abel couldn't admit anything, even if he wanted.

"Please let him go!" Hana yelled as she raced to pull Cain off her beloved. Grabbing his arm, Hana was flung aside. Landing on the grass, she twisted her ankle and squealed.

Realizing what he'd done, Cain withdrew his hand from his brother's throat. Gasping, Abel looked at his once warm and loving brother with bewildered, pained eyes.

Cain rushed to Hana's side and said, "I'm sorry... Hana, I'm so sorry."

Whimpering, she responded with spitting in his face. "I'll never marry you!" she growled. "Your brother is ten times the man you are, and I am going to have his child! It's too late! I'm completely his now!"

Cain could no longer think clearly. His jealousy overtook his entire being in a matter of seconds. Thrusting Hana down to the ground, he got on top of her and yelled, "You are mine! You will always be mine!"

Abel didn't know what to do. He didn't want to hurt his brother, but he had to stop him. Grabbing the fallen apple, he threw it at his brother's head. It was almost comical, and yet, not funny in the slightest.

Cain then turned to his brother and looked at him like a bull on the hunt. Getting up from Hana, Cain rushed over to Abel and punched him hard across the face.

The punch hit Abel like lightning. He staggered backward, unable to keep conscious. His thoughts raced: his mother, his father, his shaman... and Hana, his beautiful new love. Quickly, he fell, and fell hard. He reached out to grab the rock nearby, trying to break his fall, but he lost consciousness right beforehand, and it was too late.

Watching his brother fall over, Cain saw Abel hit his head on the rock. "Abel!" he yelled as he saw blood spatter from his brother's golden-haired head. "No!" screamed Cain as he realized the damage he unknowingly inflicted.

Hana screamed as well, and all the tribe heard. Alon came running, but it was too late. When he arrived, he saw his beloved son lying across a large rock near the apple tree. It was blood-soaked, and Abel seemed unresponsive. Alon tried to wrap his son's head with a piece of his own shirt, but the blood kept flowing.

"Wake up, Abel, please!" begged Alon. Realizing his words alone wouldn't help, he said, "Cain, go get your mother immediately! She was once a great healer! Only she will know what to do!"

Cain ran, terrified of what he'd done. As he ran, he found his mother and father who were already making their way to the apple tree.

"Is he alive?" asked Hana with tears streaming down her face.

"Yes, I think so," replied Alon, worried more than his words implied.

"Let me see my son!" commanded Eden as she rushed to Abel's side. She saw the wound on the back of his head and took a deep breath. She wouldn't let herself fall to panic before trying everything she could to save him. "The bark of the holy tree will revive him, Alon," she said with fierce eyes. "Go get it. NOW!"

Alon didn't want to leave Abel's side, but he did as his beloved queen asked. Racing to the white tree, he felt a sinking feeling. Time was against him, and he knew it. Cutting pieces of the tree with his knife, Alon wondered if Eden was right. *Can this bark really save him?* he silently asked. *Please, Sky Father, save my son. Please!*

Seconds became minutes, and minutes felt like infinity. When Alon made his way back to the apple tree, Hana was wailing, and Eden was crying over Abel's lifeless body. Cain was covering his own mouth, shocked and strangled by guilt while Adam grimaced in despair.

It was too late. *The Sky Father has rejected my prayer, but why?* Thought Alon. He then felt a deep emptiness cut through him like the rock that had cut into Abel's brain. He wanted to hate Cain, or even Adam, for putting such violence into Cain's soul, but Alon knew it wasn't truly either of their faults. It was out of their hands. He wondered it was even in the sky's control?

"Father?!" he yelled as the rest of them cried. "Have you done this to punish me?! He was young and foolish, but he was good and loving and true! Please, Father, forgive him and punish me instead! I am to blame! Take me instead, and I will never ask for anything again!"

Desperate and full of grief, Alon fell to his knees, tears streaming down his face. Eden wanted to run to her beloved, but she couldn't make herself leave Abel's side.

Surprisingly, it was Cain who knelt by Alon and said, "It was not your fault, my teacher, it was mine, and mine alone. I struck him, and I deserve whatever punishment the Father decides to give me." Getting up while wiping his tears, Cain added, "I will go far from here and never return. For what I've done, I don't deserve to be forgiven."

"No," said Adam, "no one will be punished. This was an accident, nothing more. Cain, you will not leave this tribe. That is an order!"

"No, Father," Cain stoically replied, "I cannot stay. I will never forgive myself for what I've done. I cannot be your next king, I am sorry. I must find a way to pay penance for taking my brother's life. I can't do that here. I must go."

Adam's long suppressed anger finally broke as he yelled, "You WILL stay, and you WILL take over this tribe when I am gone. Do you understand me?!"

Cain shook his head with sad eyes, and then ran... far, far into the forest.

Eden felt helpless as she lost both her sons in one day. "Go after him, Alon," she said with a broken, scratchy voice.

Alon did as she asked and chased Cain into the forest. However, the young, fit hunter didn't want to be caught, and soon, Alon lost his trail. *I have failed,* he thought as he sat on the ground, defeated.

You could become the snake again, came a voice inside his head. Unaware of what the voice meant, Alon shrugged and got back up. "No, I won't fail my queen!" he said as he stood.

Retracing his steps, he eventually found Cain. He was resting against an old, twisted tree. Alon sat next to him and held his hand. He wanted Cain to know he did not hate him, and that he still loved him, no matter what.

Opening his tear-stained eyes, Cain said, "I didn't mean to kill him. I swear I didn't."

"I know," said Alon, "and I'm sure the Sky Father will forgive you."

"I don't know if I believe the Sky Father even exists," replied Cain with a scowl. "What makes us stupid men think it's even a father? Maybe it's a mother. Maybe she became furious with me when I attacked Hana and is now punishing me by making me take my own brother's life."

"I don't know," said Alon. "Maybe you're right... or maybe it's neither he nor she. Maybe the sky is just the sky and doesn't judge one way or another."

Cain nodded, confused. Unable to keep it in, he broke into tears and went into Alon's chest. "I'm so sorry, Teacher! I know he was really your son... and you loved him dearly. Please, forgive me."

Alon sobbed along with Cain, holding him tight. After they cried, he said, "It's alright, my boy. I forgive you, but can you forgive yourself?"

Cain sniffed and said, "I don't know."

"Then that will be your test," said Alon, "which will not be given to you by the sky, but by your own heart."

Cain nodded, then rose to his feet and said, "Please look after my mother, and everyone."

"Where are you going?" asked Alon, deeply concerned.

"I don't know, but I know the sky will light my way. Thank you, Teacher... for everything."

Cain then walked into the dark of the forest, alone and unafraid. Alon was afraid for him, but he knew he could not stop him any more than he could stop the moon from glowing brightly in the night-sky.

Days passed by, and after Abel's funeral and Cain's departure, the tribe was never quite the same. There had been a killing, even if accidental, and it was a horrific, unnatural act that had never occurred before. The fact that it had happened to the blessed, royal family made the horror even worse. No one could understand how and why such a terrible thing could happen.

People whispered that Cain had gone mad when his jealousy took over his mind, but it still didn't quite answer the riddle. No one knew who to blame or how to feel. Some blamed Hana, but others defended her.

Hana herself wanted to be left alone. Every day, she brought flowers and fruits to Abel's grave by the apple tree. She hoped the tree would become even stronger, and with each apple that bloomed, Abel would live on.

She soon gave birth to their son, and she named him Seth. His name meant "Anointed Child." It was her way of publicly declaring her love for Abel and to prove their love had been holy and fated.

Even at his birth, she asked Queen Eden to anoint him with water and apple seeds, unknowingly creating a ritual to come for many years. The ritual, along with her strong words and fierce pride, made Hana quite popular within the tribe, and soon, she had replaced Eden as their ideal of motherly love.

The tribe blossomed again as time and love healed their inner wounds. There were casualties from the fallen fruit of Eden's womb, but most moved on.

Adam, unable to lead, stepped down as Hana was named Queen with her son being raised as the next king. Adam changed and took a spiritual turn, finally taking on the role of Shaman, which he hoped would make the spirit of his father proud.

Eden found herself mentoring Hana, though she had no doubt the tribe's new queen could handle herself. She was strong, outspoken, and even the hunters believed in her judgement.

As Eden grew old, she felt it was time for her to rest. Having no idea where Alon had gone since the day he left to find Cain, she was now alone, and she craved only one person: her beautiful white serpent from long ago.

Sneaking away from the tribe, she slowly walked toward her holy tree, which had grown enormous since she had seen it last. In the glistening sunlight, she recalled the first moment she had seen her sweet serpentine friend. She was filled with melancholia as she sat down and remembered giving birth to her first son.

"Why has he not returned, Old Tree?" she asked. "Why could he not fight his envy with love?"

Knowing the tree would not answer, she fell asleep. Soon, the sky began to drip, as if it were releasing tiny tears. It didn't wake her, though, for sadness and age kept her from opening her eyes.

However, the serpent hanging in the tree opened his eyes, for he had recognized his old love. *Was it a dream that I loved her? He asked himself. No... it couldn't have been a dream. I remember the feel of her skin and the softness of her voice. Oh yes, I remember now... it was when I was a man, and I thought I could help them to understand the world of colors. How silly I was to think such a thing when I barely understood it myself.*

Just then, Eden awoke, as if she somehow heard his thoughts. "My serpent," she said, rising to her feet while searching the branches with her hands, "is that you?"

"Yes, my sweet queen, it is me," he replied. "I am glad you can still understand me, even though I have changed back into a snake."

"What do you mean? What were you before?"

"I was a man. Don't you remember me?"

Taking a moment, she saw Alon's face in her mind, and she exhaled in realization. "Oh, my sweet love! What happened to you the day you ran after Cain? Why did you leave me?"

"I'm sorry, my love," he said as he slithered up to her face. "I didn't mean to leave you. I was very upset that day. I couldn't stop Cain from leaving us. I felt defeated, and I gave up. I blamed myself for everything that went wrong, and it was in that moment of self-hate that I found myself reverted back into the serpent form I am now. I suppose I didn't know why I was a man any longer, and so I lost the ability to stay with you. I'm sorry."

"Oh, Alon... my poor, beloved serpent," she cried as she stroked his head. "You sacrificed so much to be with us. Why did you do it in the first place? Were you not happy living as a snake surrounded by nature?"

"No, I wanted to be with you, my love," he sweetly replied. "I felt called to you, though it was more than that. I wanted..."

"Yes?"

"I wanted to teach people about the rainbow."

"The rainbow?" she asked, intrigued. "I don't recall you teaching about that when you were our Shaman."

"I know," he replied while slithering around her shoulders, "I became so caught up in the daily pains and joys of living as a man, I forgot the true reason I was there. I wasted time, and now, I barely remember what it was about the rainbow that I even wanted to teach. I have failed... everyone."

"No, Alon," she hushed, petting his head, "you did not fail. You taught me about love and how to be strong."

"You knew that all along, my queen," he replied with a smile. However, his smile slowly turned to a fear-filled frown as he saw her begin to lose consciousness. "No, please don't go yet, my love," he begged her. "I'm not ready to say goodbye!"

"I'm sorry, my beloved Alon," she whispered as she slowly lowered to the ground. "I am old, and unlike you, I am not a magical creature who can defy age. I must sleep the eternal sleep... and maybe I will see our sweet son in the dream world."

Alon cried, but accepted her words as truth. "Yes, I am sure you will see him. Please, tell Abel how much I love him."

"I will," she replied with a smile. "Goodbye, my beloved serpent. I will see you again soon."

Her hand then fell from his head, and he was left on her motionless lap to ponder the meaning of his life.

Without his Eden, he no longer wished to live. He didn't believe in the "Father" any longer – only the emotionless, selfish sky – so he had no one to listen to his prayers.

Why am I here?! he shouted in his mind. *I'm neither a snake nor a man! It's not fair! I do not understand why I am so pale... so translucent! No wonder she could not be with me! I have no colors at all! How can I teach anyone about something I know nothing about?! I am a fake! I am a fool!"*

The rain fell harder as Alon began to sing a song for his queen. He sang about love, longing, pain, and death, and the song was so beautiful that the other animals nearby came to listen.

Soon, the sky cleared, and the rain stopped falling. The light of the sun peered through the clouds and beamed directly onto the pale snake's skin.

Then, the animals all gasped in awe. Even the king of the elephants came to get a closer look and was amazed.

Noticing the animals were staring at him, he asked, "What is it? Why are you all looking at me so?"

"Can you not see yourself?" asked the elephant king. "Look at your skin, my friend, then look above you! It is glorious!"

Alon looked at his usually pale skin and saw something amazing. The water had mixed with his translucent scales, and had created a beautiful, shiny rainbow! Almost in tears, Alon looked above him and saw what the elephant king had seen: it was a giant, arched rainbow in the sky! His own skin was reflecting the colors above!

"Look, Eden!" he shouted in joy. "I am the rainbow after all!"

Laughing and crying, the serpent understood what he was meant to do. The sky had always known, and had always told him. The colors were always there, but he had to be willing to see them. They were not just on his skin, but inside him, and inside everyone—connected together in a great circle of diversity and love. Finally, Alon realized what evolving truly meant.

Knowing he wasn't the immortal being Eden had assumed he was, he closed his eyes and let his body sleep alongside his queen. The animals all cried, and from then on, they never forgot how the Rainbow Serpent and his woman joined as one by the ancient tree of light.

The humans remembered as well, though they recalled it as "The Apple Tree of Knowledge," and they passed on their story of love, envy, and death to their offspring for hundreds of years. Yet, it was not merely a cautionary tale, for there was a hidden meaning within.

In time, however, many meanings were lost. Eden's name was changed to hide her love for her snake, and most forgot the truth behind their beloved garden.

As the years passed, only the wisest remembered that there is no blessed or cursed, saint or sinner, chosen or fallen. There is only truth and the colors of the rainbow.

Lyra Shanti

If you enjoyed this book, please leave a review!

The Rainbow Serpent on Amazon.com

More Books by Lyra Shanti

Shiva XIV

Books 1-4 of this epic Sci-Fi Series

The Artist

Can love save a man from himself?

Sediments

The Selected Poems of Lyra Shanti

All books on paperback and Kindle at

www.amazon.com

Lyra Shanti is a novelist, playwright, poet, and songwriter who currently resides in Florida with partner and spouse, Timothy Casey, and their two crazy cats.

For more information about Lyra Shanti, go to: LyraShanti.com